PROPERTY OF

"WE ARE SUCH STUFF AS DREAMS
ARE MADE ON; AND OUR LITTLE
LIFE IS ROUNDED WITH A SLEEP."

—*The Tempest*, act 4, scene 1

DATE

"Men at some time are masters of their fates.
The fault, dear Brutus, is not in our stars,
but in ourselves, that we are underlings."

—*JULIUS CAESAR*, ACT 1, SCENE 2

DATE

"ALL THE WORLD'S A STAGE,
AND ALL THE MEN AND
WOMEN MERELY PLAYERS."
—*As You Like It*, act 2, scene 7

"LIVE A LITTLE; COMFORT A LITTLE;
CHEER THYSELF A LITTLE."

—*As You Like It*, act 2, scene 6

"Our doubts are traitors and make us lose the
good we oft might win by fearing to attempt."

—*MEASURE FOR MEASURE*, ACT 1, SCENE 4

"GOOD COMPANY, GOOD WINE,
GOOD WELCOME
CAN MAKE GOOD PEOPLE."
—*Henry VIII*, act 1, scene 4

"Have more than thou showest,
speak less than thou knowest."

—*KING LEAR*, ACT 1, SCENE 4

DATE

"SELF-LOVE, MY LIEGE, IS NOT SO
VILE A SIN, AS SELF-NEGLECTING."

—*Henry V*, act 2, scene 4

"LOVE ALL, TRUST A FEW,
DO WRONG TO NONE."

—*All's Well That Ends Well*, act 1, scene 1

"There is nothing either good or bad
that thinking makes it so."

—*HAMLET*, ACT 2, SCENE 2

"MAKE NOT YOUR
THOUGHTS YOUR PRISONS."

—*Antony and Cleopatra*, act 5, scene 2

"*The web of our life is of a mingled yarn,
good and ill together.*"

—*ALL'S WELL THAT ENDS WELL*, ACT 4, SCENE 3

"WISELY AND SLOW;
THEY STUMBLE THAT RUN FAST."

—*Romeo and Juliet*, act 2, scene 3

DATE

"There are more things in heaven and earth,
Horatio, than are dreamt of in your philosophy."
—*HAMLET*, ACT 1, SCENE 5

"AND THOUGH SHE BE BUT
LITTLE, SHE IS FIERCE."
—*A Midsummer Night's Dream*,
act 3, scene 2

DATE

"WE KNOW WHAT WE ARE, BUT
KNOW NOT WHAT WE MAY BE."
—*Hamlet*, act 4, scene 5

DATE

"There is a tide in the affairs of men, which,
taken at the flood, leads on to fortune."

—*JULIUS CAESAR*, ACT 4, SCENE 3

"IF I LOSE MINE HONOR,
I LOSE MYSELF."

—*Antony and Cleopatra*, act 3, scene 4

DATE _____

DATE

"A fool doth think he is wise, but the wise
man knows himself to be a fool."

—*AS YOU LIKE IT*, ACT 5, SCENE 1